PABLO & HIS CHAIR

DELPHINE PERRET

WITHDRAWN

PRINCETON ARCHITECTURAL PRESS

NEW YORK

Today is the first day of autumn.

That's what the newspapers said on the morning of Pablo's birthday. They did not mention, however, the little scab on Pablo's knee, which he got from falling on the gravel. Neither did they mention his victory at the soccer game the day before, nor the fact that it was his birthday. But his birthday was, of course, the most important event of the day.

The little scab was not so important—he'd added it to the one on his shin. And the ones on his elbow and forearm. And those on his chin, ankle, and wrist.

Pablo was a stunt boy, but only on certain days. Most of the time he was a student, a kid, a musician, an astronaut, a cowboy, or a soccer player.

That day there was no school. And Pablo, after he blew out the candles on the cake they would eat for the rest of the week, received a well-wrapped present. He tore the paper away as his grandmother watched, teary-eyed.

"A chair?"

Yes, a chair. Who had ever gotten a chair for their birthday?

Who would think up such a present?

Why would anyone give a person a chair for their birthday?

"So you'll sit still for once!"

Pablo was so flabbergasted, he didn't even notice who made this little comment.

So he took the chair and shut himself in his bedroom, angry.

He glared at it. He stuck his tongue out at it.

He scratched the seat a little, just to see.

After one hour, he was balancing on it. After two hours,
he was doing a handstand. And by the end of the day, he was
a skilled chair acrobat.

A few days later he was seen leaving his room with the chair on his back. He crossed the living room, opened the front door, and turned to give a big wave goodbye.

Then he set off quickly down the road.

The dirt from the road got into his socks.

He walked through one town, stopped at the next one,
then left two days later for another. He went on this way
until he reached the other end of the country.

And there, on the terrace of a cafe,
he started performing a balancing act.
A passerby stopped to watch. Then two.
Then ten. He finished his act to the
applause of the crowd. He was pleased.

He went on and walked across the next
country. Then the next, and then another.

People would give him the money in their
pockets. The money for their bread—never
mind, they would eat tomorrow. The
money for the two pounds of tomatoes
for their summer soup. The money
to buy their shoe polish.

Theaters and performance halls soon started asking for Pablo. They put up posters with his name, announcing his tour. People fought to get tickets, to be amazed by his daring show. Front-row seats were the best—so close you could count his eyelashes.

All the world hoped
to have a chance to see him
perform. He bought himself
a beautiful stage costume.
He was the best act in all
of the most famous
festivals and the most
prestigious shows.

He walked across huge cities where nobody ever sleeps, rubbed shoulders with performing lions and famous pianists, had breakfast with a czar, rode in a hot air balloon, swam in a river in Finland, and received never-ending applause in the most beautiful theaters in the world.

In the mornings he sipped tea and ate toast. He had remained humble and was enjoying every moment. Despite the chic hotels, glitz, and glamour, he could still appreciate the sound of a dragonfly and the cool wind in his hair.

And then one day, he put his chair on his back again, left the hotel room, went across the lobby, opened the door, and set off quickly down the road.

He walked for a long time, smiling as he passed by the cities he had crossed a few years earlier. He climbed up hills, descended into valleys, walked along cliffs, stopped to rest a little, and continued onward.
He never looked back.

The road slipped a bit of dirt into his socks.

Before he knew it, he saw his house up ahead.

He went in without knocking. Everybody was around the table.

"There you are!"

A plate was waiting for him; only a chair was missing.

"I have a lot to tell you!"

And for the first time, Pablo pulled his chair underneath him and sat down.